Wally's Wish

ISBN-13: 978-1-63587-279-8
ISBN-10: 1-635872-79-0

Visit us at www.biancaryans.com

Acknowledgement: First and foremost, I would like to thank my mother, Johnett, for always encouraging me throughout the course of my life. I would not be where I am today without her. I also want to thank my brother, Malik, for being an amazing support system. My family has been there for me throughout this entire journey and have shared in my excitement. My close friends have given me the courage to go after what I want and I am so grateful to have them in my life. Lastly, I want to thank Troika Publishing for giving me this amazing opportunity to make my dreams come true.
This book would not be possible without the help of these very special people.

Dedication: To my late father, Narvis Ray Ryans who taught me that anything is possible if you believe in yourself and work hard.

All his life, Wally was told by his parents that soon he would become a beautiful butterfly. He waited and wished for that day to come, but it never did.

Wally saw all of his caterpillar friends turn into these beautiful creatures. They seemed so perfect, flying through the air with their colorful wings. They teased and taunted him because he took so long to change. Some said he'd be an ugly caterpillar forever.

Every time one of the caterpillars turned into
a butterfly, they would fly away into the trees
and leave Wally. Soon, Wally was all alone in
the bottom of the forest.

Wally was so sad that he hadn't changed yet.
He was still an ugly, hairy caterpillar, and now
he was all alone while everyone else flew freely
as beautiful creatures.

As weeks passed and Wally still didn't change, he began to think that he would never be with his friends and he gave up on his wish to become a beautiful butterfly.

One day, Wally saw a caterpillar sitting on a leaf. He wasn't alone anymore! He asked the caterpillar, "Why haven't we changed yet? Isn't that what caterpillars are supposed to do?"

The lady caterpillar told him, "I'll show you how we change! It takes times and hard work to become a beautiful creature. Since you took the most time to change, I'm sure you will be the most beautiful butterfly in the whole forest!"

Together, they climbed up a strong leaf and the lady caterpillar showed Wally how to form a cocoon.

They stayed in the cocoon for what seemed like years to Wally, but when they broke out, Wally was the most beautiful caterpillar anyone had ever seen. They admired Wally's beautiful wings and apologized for teasing him for taking so long to change.

They flew together with all of the other butterflies in the forest. Wally and his butterfly friends lived together in the forest happily.

About the author: Bianca Ryans is a fifteen year-old writer and
artist who lives in California. Her goal is to inspire people
through her words and artwork. Bianca was inspired to write
Wally's Wish because as a teenager, it can be difficult to figure
out who you want to be as an adult while you are still so young.
Wally's Wish is a coming of age story, encouraging children to
take their time growing up. After all, the more time spent in
childhood will result in a very well-rounded adult.

Visit Bianca at www.biancaryans.com